SOCKS ROCK!

A Collection of
SERIOUSLY
SILLY
SOCK
STORIES

Barbara Steele

ISBN: 1439248591
ISBN-13: 9781439248591

Library of Congress Control Number: 2009906666

DEDICATION

To my son, Cody, the coolest kid ever—you knock my socks off! Thank you for inspiring these stories. I love you to the universe and back... and forth!

To my mom, the beautiful soul who continues to inspire me from the great beyond to live every day with imagination, optimism and vigor.

To my dad, from whom my "silliness" genes come from, no doubt. I love you so much, Dad!

To my siblings, extended family and friends, for always reminding me to never stop loving, laughing and dreaming. I love you all very much!

CONTENTS

INTRODUCTION

I'll never forget the fun that my son, Cody, and I used to have when he was just six years old. We had evening sessions of silliness before bed, throwing socks around and spontaneously reciting made-up poems.

One night, after a good case of the giggles and sock talk, we talked about turning the poems into a book someday. We even discussed the good that could come of it. We decided that if we someday made any money from the stories, we would give back to someone in need. With that said, a percentage of the proceeds from the sale of this book will be donated for the purchase of socks and shoes for homeless children.

I hope that you and your children will find as much pleasure and love in reading these sock stories as Cody and I found in creating them.

FRED

I took off one sock
on my way to the bed.
"Oh, my gosh!"
It flew over my head!

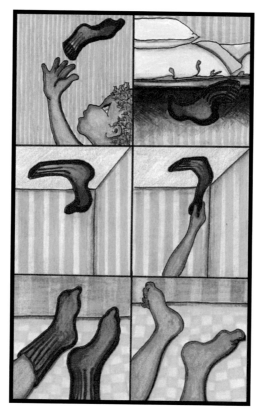

It flew up in the air
then flipped under the bed.
Then it suddenly said,
that his name was Fred!

I climbed out of the bed
to look under at Fred.
I had to be sure
I had heard what he said!

Fred yelled, "Oh my!"
and sprang up with a cry.
He got stuck on the ceiling.
He was up really high!

So I reached over my head
and pulled Fred to the bed,
then, happily, I said,
"THANK YOU, Fred!"

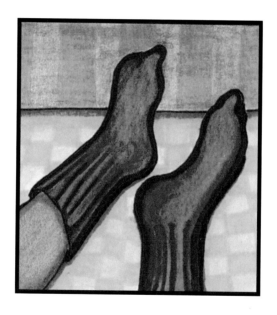

So I put Fred back on
and fell asleep with a yawn.
When I woke up at dawn,
my socks WERE BOTH GONE!

THE SOCK MONSTER

I know there's a sock monster.
Really, I do!
It lives under the dryer,
or inside my shoe.

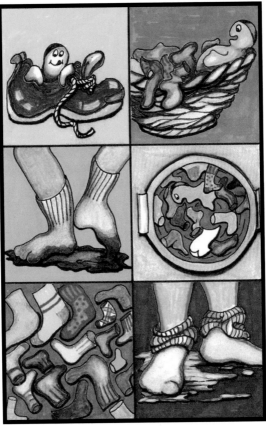

When my mom does the laundry,
as clean as can be...
when she can't find a sock,
she just yells at me!

But I never have it.
Really, I don't!
I say, "Ask the sock monster!"
but she says that she won't.

I start out with both socks
upon my two feet.
Then I get them all muddy,
because mud's really neat!

The next thing I know,
Mom takes the socks off my feet.
They go into the washer,
which makes them smell sweet.

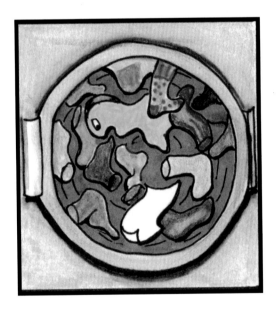

Next step's the dryer
with a fresh dryer sheet.
And that's when the monster
decides that SOCKS ARE TO EAT!.

Now there's rarely a time
when mom's socks and mine
come out as a pair
when she removes them from there!

So, don't you forget!
You should never ever let
mom put your socks in the dryer.
You should JUST WEAR THEM WET!

THERE'S A HOLE IN MY SOLE!

There's a hole in my sole
and it's taking a toll
on the sore that I have on my heel.

My torn socks, you see.
are frustrating me,
and my blister just won't seem to heal.

It all started today
when I was outside to play
and I saw my Pap's prize fishing reel.

I looked right, I looked left.
I didn't consider it theft.
I figured I'd just make a deal.

So I slipped off my shoes.
I had nothing to lose!
I replaced the torn socks for the reel.

But before I departed
I finished the note I had started
to write, to tell Pap of the deal.

Then I realized I forgot
to leave the note behind, in the spot
where I had left the socks for the reel.

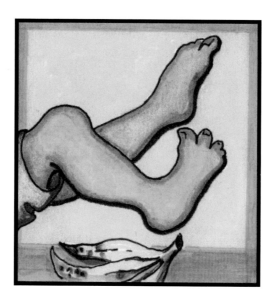

I ran back to the spot very fast
and almost had reached it at last,
when I slipped on a banana peel!

Then I heard my pants rip
just as my Pap got a grip
on the socks I had left for his reel.

When I tried to explain
what had happened that day.
My Pap didn't seem to agree.

Since the note wasn't there.
it was tough to be fair,
so he just sighed as he
TOOK BACK HIS REEL!

THE SOCK BAND

There once was a rock-and-roll band
that jammed with a sock on each hand.

And even with the socks,
they all sounded quite good.
With all of that fuzz,
you'd never think that they would!

The lead guitar player
had a very young son.
His fear of loud music often
caused him to run.
To the closet he went,
with a hand on each ear.
Loud music had caused this
young boy so much fear.

The band members thought
about what could be done
to turn all the music into
something that's fun.

They thought and they thought,
and with a little confusion
a warm, cuddly, sock had
become their solution.

Each band member bent over
to take off their shoes
You can surely imagine,
they had nothing to lose!

The socks did the trick,
because they muffled the sound.
Since the boy's fear was gone, he now
JAMMED WITH THE BAND!

SOCK IT TO ME!

SOCKS ROCK!

Cody had a blue sock and
Anna had a red sock.
Ryan had a new sock and
Austin had a few socks.
ONE DAY...
Cody wanted a new sock and
Anna needed a blue sock
Ryan wanted one more sock and
Austin was missing two socks!
NOW, IMAGINE
WHAT WOULD HAPPEN...
IF NOBODY SHARED?

Cody would **take** Ryan's new sock
and Anna would **sneak** Cody's blue sock!

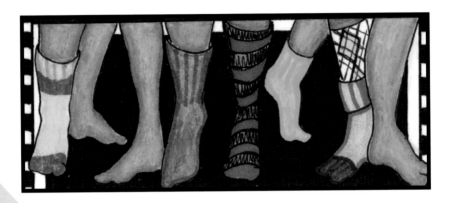

AND THEN...

Ryan would **grab** Austin's few socks
and Austin would **snatch** Anna's red sock!

WHAT A MESS IT WOULD BE!
TURN THE PAGE, AND YOU'LL SEE...

Socks would be
flying **everywhere**!
Red and blue socks would
be up in the **air**!

OH, NO!

New socks would **all**
end up with a **tear**...
and **all** of the socks would
be in need of **repairs**!

BUT WHAT IF THEY ALL
DECIDED TO SHARE?

Cody would end up with a NEW sock
and Anna would have a BRIGHT BLUE sock.

THAT'S NOT ALL...

Ryan would have
MORE THAN A FEW socks
and Austin would have
RED, WHITE AND BLUE SOCKS!

NOBODY WOULD HAVE
A MATCHING PAIR,
BUT THEY'D ALL BE
SO MUCH HAPPIER,
AFTER THEY SHARED!

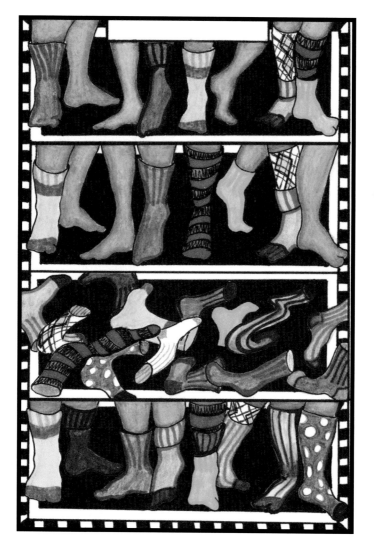

64965477R00018

Made in the USA
Middletown, DE
21 February 2018